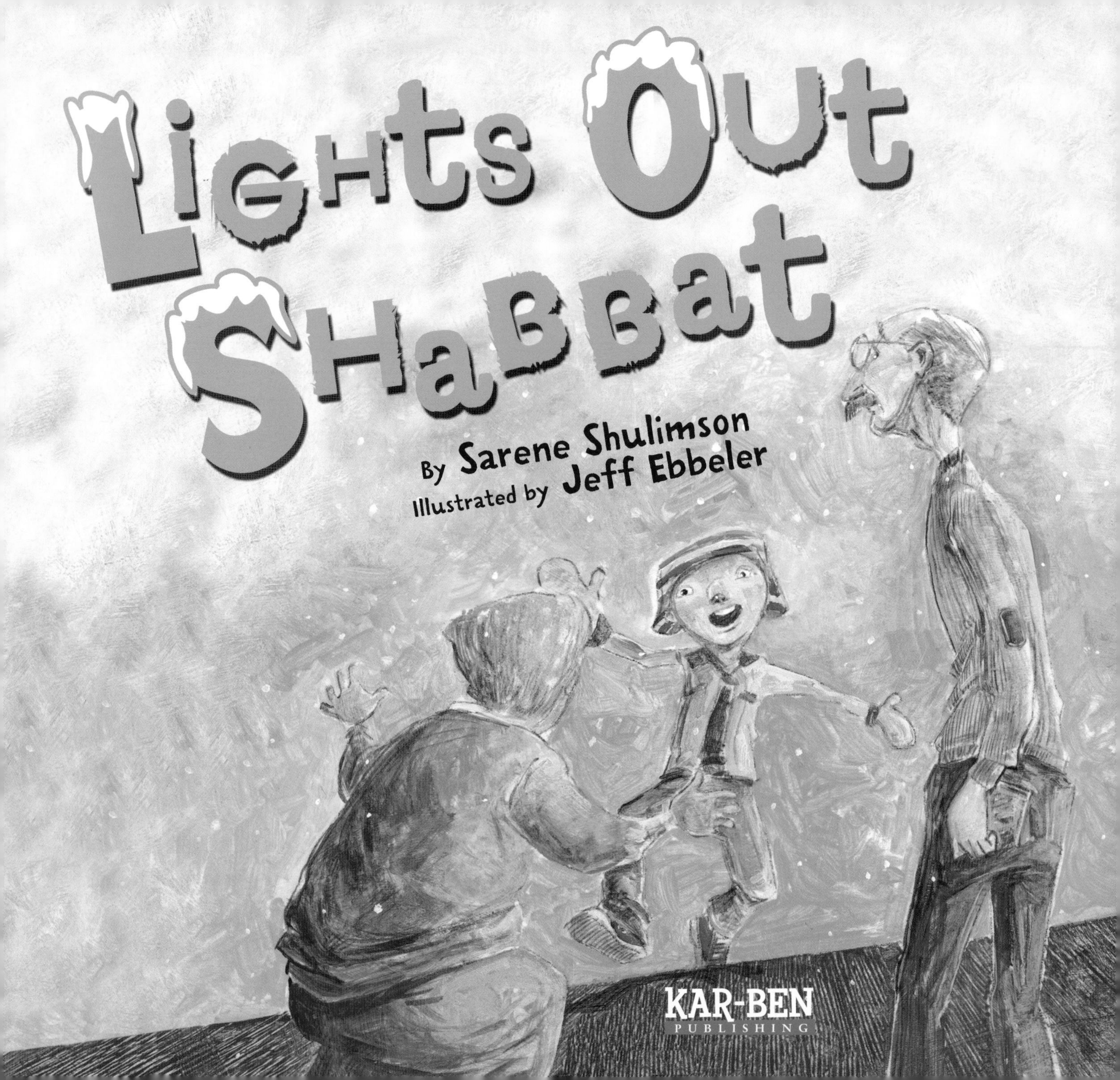
Lights Out Shabbat
By Sarene Shulimson
Illustrated by Jeff Ebbeler
KAR-BEN
PUBLISHING

It doesn't snow in Georgia very often. But one Friday night it did. I was sleeping over at my Nana and Papa's house.

The snow started at night, right after we lit the Shabbat candles. Then the lights went out. I wasn't scared, because we were all together.

We had a yummy Shabbat dinner. Cold grape juice, warm challah, cheese blintzes, and lettuce from the garden. Then we ate cherry snow cones!

But the lights did not come on.

Papa told me stories about when he was a little boy. The Shabbat candles burned low.

I snuggled close to him and felt very sleepy. I dreamed the snow was a warm fuzzy blanket.

In the morning, the sun was bright. Birds sang outside my window, but the house was very quiet. The electricity was still not working. Nana and I said a special prayer thanking God for our good night's sleep, and for waking up healthy in the morning. And for keeping the house warm.

But the lights did not come on.

Nana and I went outside to make snowmen.

Nana made a snow dog.

I held her hand as we walked around the neighborhood.

When we came back, my snowman had shrunk, standing shorter in the grass. Nana's snow dog had run away.

My snowman disappeared while I was taking a Shabbat nap. Outside the grass was wet and the air was chilly. Inside, I played with Daddy's and Papa's old toys in the attic. Soon the house began to get dark.

But the lights did not come on.

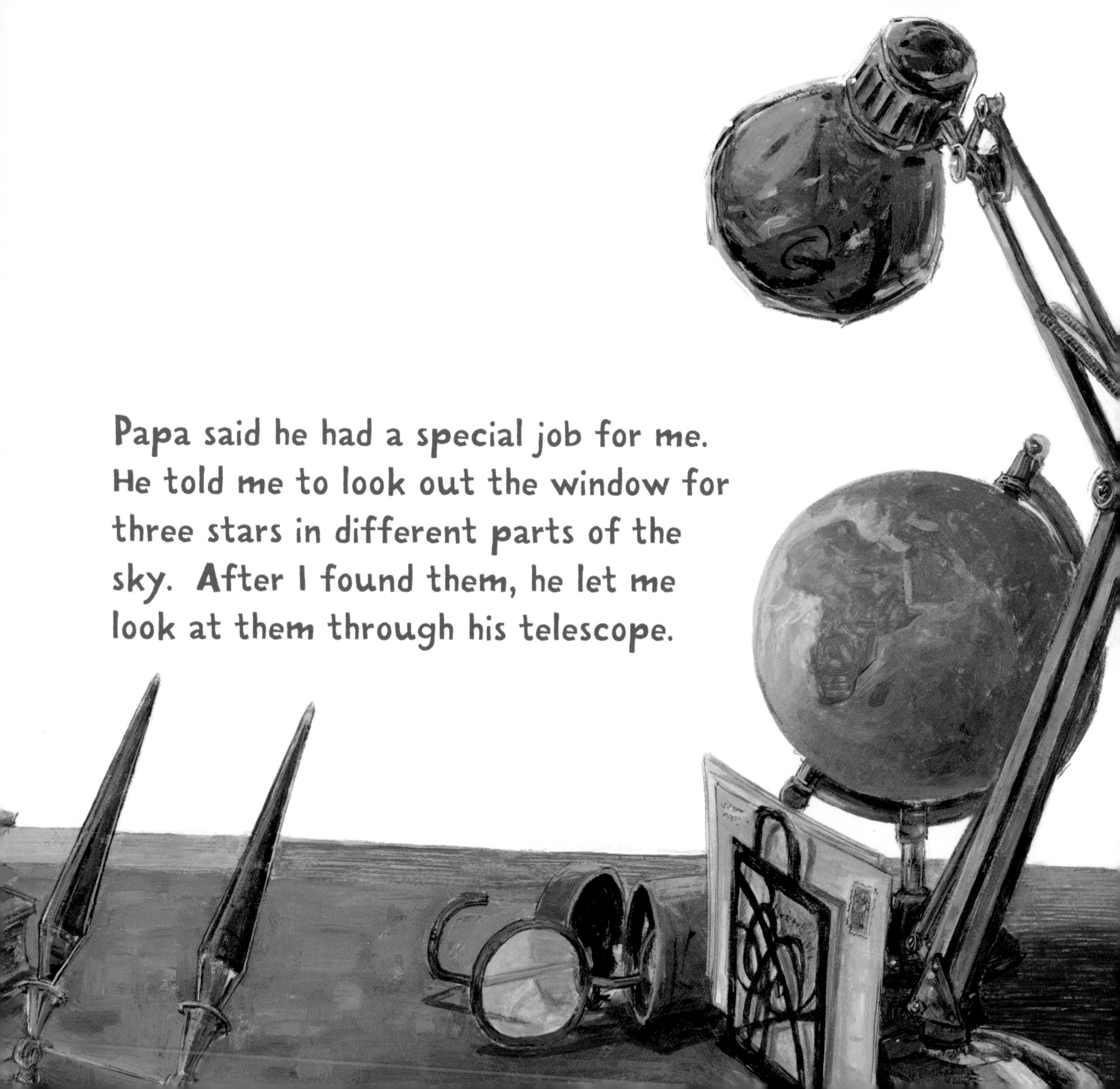

Papa said he had a special job for me. He told me to look out the window for three stars in different parts of the sky. After I found them, he let me look at them through his telescope.

"Now you can help me say havdalah," said Papa. A special silver wine cup sat on the table. Nana poured some grape juice.

Papa said the blessing over wine. "Thank you, God, for making all things exist."

"Like snow in Georgia," I added.

Nana handed me the beautiful silver spicebox. I closed my eyes and took a deep breath to hold in as many sweet smells of Shabbat as I could. "Thank you, God," we said, "for creating wonderful spices."

Papa lit a large braided candle. Nana showed me how to make shadows on my hands from the candlelight. My fingernails looked bright like stars twinkling in the sky.

We said a prayer and Papa put out the flame with a drop of wine. The candle hissed and curly gray wisps rose from the wicks.

But the lights did not come on.

The moonlight came
through the window.
Shabbat was over.
Papa gave me a hug.
“Shavuah Tov,” he said.
“Have a good week.”

All of a sudden, the room was so bright I had to blink. The refrigerator began to hum. All the sounds of the house returned.

And the lights came on.

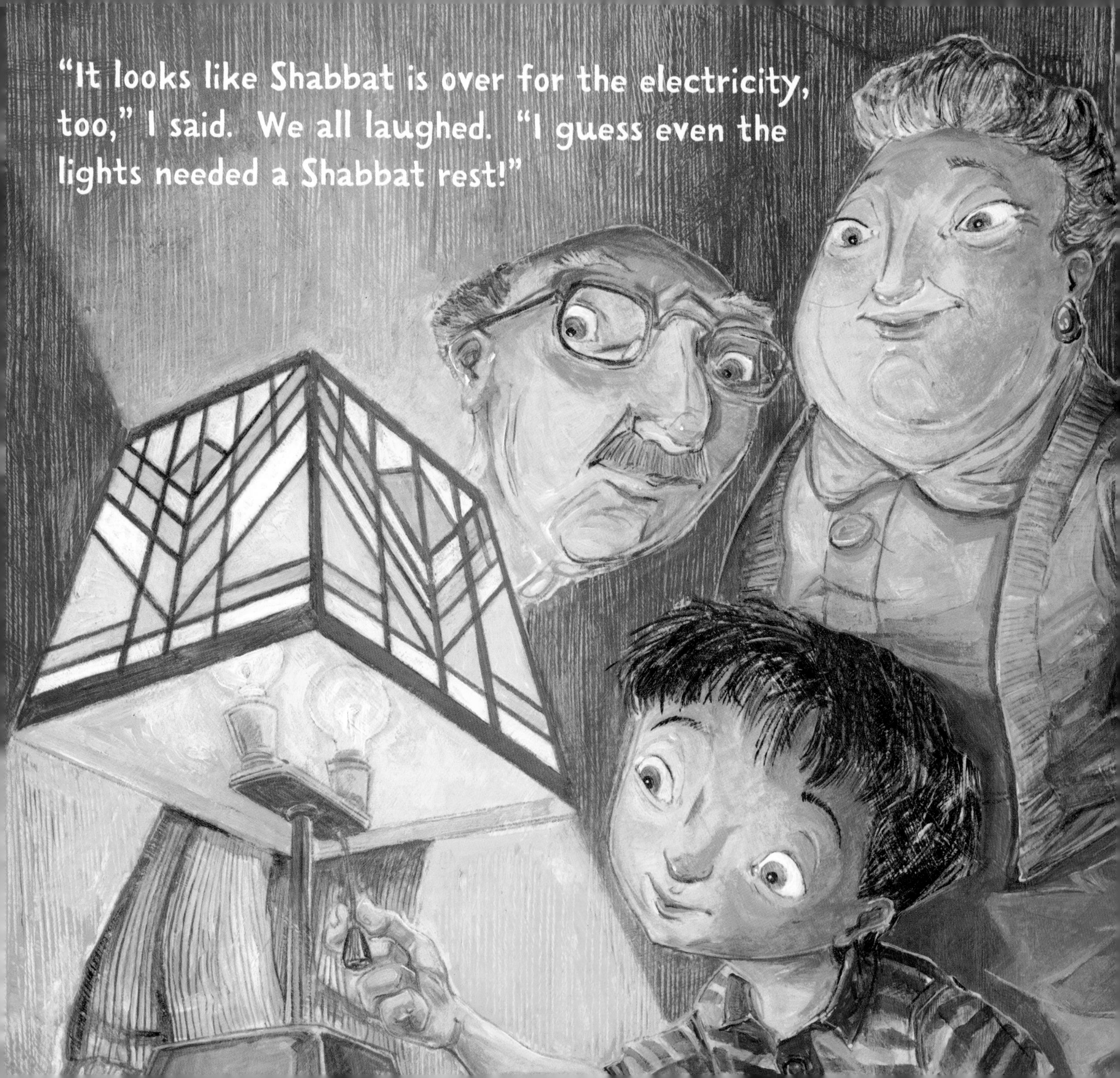

"It looks like Shabbat is over for the electricity, too," I said. We all laughed. "I guess even the lights needed a Shabbat rest!"

With love to my support and inspirations, Dan, Jarrod, Ari, and Lily,
and to my own grandparents, Mama Ida, Papa Dan, Mama Frances
and Papa Sam—you are forever in my heart— S.S.

KAR-BEN Publishing
A division of Lerner Publishing Group, Inc.
241 First Avenue North
Minneapolis, MN 55401 U.S.A.
800-4KARBEN

Website address: www.karben.com

Library of Congress Cataloging-in-Publication Data

Shulimson, Sarene.
Lights out Shabbat / by Sarene Shulimson ; illustrated by Jeff Ebbeler.
p. cm.
Summary: A grandchild spending the weekend with Nana and Papa celebrates Shabbat during a rare Georgia snowfall when the power goes out.
ISBN: 978-0-7613-7564-7 (lib. bdg. : alk. paper)
[1. Sabbath—Fiction. 2. Grandparents—Fiction. 3. Judaism—Customs and practices—Fiction. 4. Snow—Fiction. 5. Georgia—Fiction.] I. Ebbeler, Jeffrey, ill. II. Title.
PZ7.S559415Li 2012
[E]—dc23 2011018986

Manufactured in Hong Kong
2-41881-12163-4/22/2016

101620.7K2/B0905/A3

Lights Out Shabbat

This
PJ BOOK
belongs to

JEWISH BEDTIME STORIES and SONGS